Sticky, Sticky, Stuck!

Written by Michael Gutch • Illustrated by Steve Björkman

HARPER

An Imprint of HarperCollinsPublishers

To my dad, who doesn't like little sticky hands,
and my mom & Di, who encourage them
—M.G.

For everyone in the "Circle of Trust." Stuck together for life!
—S.B.

Sticky, Sticky, Stuck!
Text copyright © 2013 by Michael Gutch
Illustrations copyright © 2013 by Steve Björkman
All rights reserved. Manufactured in China.
No part of this book may be used or reproduced in any manner whatsoever without
written permission except in the case of brief quotations embodied in critical articles and reviews.
For information address HarperCollins Children's Books, a division of HarperCollins Publishers,
10 East 53rd Street, New York, NY 10022.
www.harpercollinschildrens.com

Library of Congress Cataloging-in-Publication Data is available.
ISBN 978-0-06-199818-8 (trade bdg.)

Typography by Jeanne L. Hogle
13 14 15 16 17 SCP 10 9 8 7 6 5 4 3 2 1
❖
First Edition

Annie's family was always busy.

Annie's dad always seemed to be typing away on his thingamajig.

Her mom was always on the computer.

If Annie's brother wasn't listening to music, he was battling aliens.

Her sister was always on her cell phone with one of her eighty closest friends.

Sometimes it seemed like no one had time for Annie.
Except to tell her that she was sticky!

"Annie, don't play with your gum!"

Even Annie's brother and sister thought she was sticky.

"EWww, Annie, that's so gross!"

"Mommm, Annie is ruining my collage!"

"One, two, three, four, I declare a thumb war. . . ."

"Yuck!

If you don't wash your hands,
I'm not playing anymore."

No matter where she was or what she was
doing, it seemed that Annie was always sticky!

Every time Annie's mom and dad told her to wash her hands, it seemed as if she never heard them. Maybe her ears were clogged with marshmallow goop.

One day Annie was hungry
and went looking for a snack.
As usual, everyone was doing
their own thing, and there was
no one to help Annie.

With such a busy family, Annie figured she would take matters into her own hands. She would make her favorite sandwich all by herself: PEANUT BUTTER AND HONEY ON WHITE BREAD.

Annie was about to grab a knife but remembered
just in time that she was not allowed to use knives.
Annie climbed up on a kitchen chair to get the
peanut butter and thought about how else she could
spread the honey and layer the peanut butter.

As she wiped her nose, it came to her! She got an idea.

Annie spread the peanut butter.
She smeared the honey.
And just as she smashed the
two pieces of bread together . . .

Annie was so surprised that she jumped up and
fell onto the dog.
 When Annie tried to get off the dog, she couldn't.

SHE WAS STUCK!

Her mom tried pulling her off the dog,
but as soon as she touched Annie, she
got stuck, too!
Annie's mother yelled to her father,

"HELP, we're stuck!"

But when Annie's father came running in, he tripped over the chair and fell onto Annie, her mother, and the dog. Her brother heard the hullabaloo and came running in. Annie's brother laughed so hard that he fell right on top of the pile. When he tried to get up, he stopped laughing. Annie's brother was stuck too!

Just then her sister walked in.

"DON'T MOVE!" shouted Dad to Annie's sister.

"Get a bucket of water!" shouted Mom.

"Throw it on us!" shouted Annie's brother.

Annie's sister dumped the water on them and then tried to pull them apart, but soon . . .

. . . she was stuck too.

The more Annie's family struggled to get unstuck, the more stuck together they became.

They all looked at one another and tried to figure out what to do.

"HELP!"

"WOOF, WOOF!"

Everyone started to complain.

"I need to call work right away!"

"I have to meet my friends."

"your breath smells like onions."

"If you had just helped Annie with her sandwich . . ."

Finally, when everyone was too tired to grumble anymore, Annie whispered, "I have an idea. Dad, can you reach the phone?"

Dad grabbed the phone with his mouth.

Mom turned it on with her nose.

"Dial the fire department!" Annie told her brother and sister. Annie's brother used his elbow and her sister used her toes! They pushed . . . and poked . . . and pressed . . . and finally, by working together, they were able to call the fire department.

"WE'RE STUCK!!!!!"

they all shouted into the phone.

"The fire department will be there in five minutes," the dispatcher said.

Annie's family celebrated and congratulated one another on working together to call the fire department. They even tried to high-five one another, which didn't really work. But they didn't care!

Five minutes later, the fire captain arrived.
He wondered why Annie's family all had smiles
on their faces.

The fire captain roared to his crew to bring in the hose.
They hosed down Annie's family.
They used soap and warm water.
After twenty minutes, the captain and his crew were
able to loosen a leg here and an arm over there . . .

But to their surprise, every time they'd free an arm, it would wrap itself back around someone else. And every time they'd loosen a leg, it would find itself twisting around another leg.

The fire captain shook his head and asked, "What's going on here? Every time we pull you people apart, you go right back to sticking together."

"Thank you, Captain, for your help, but I don't think that we really want to be unstuck yet,"

Annie's father said.

"I can text my friends later," her sister said.

"This is a lot better than a video game," her brother added.

"Work can wait," Annie's dad said happily.

"So can dinner," Mom finished.

The fire captain soon got the picture. He gathered his equipment and crew and happily left the house, knowing that his job was done.

Annie didn't feel hungry anymore.
And for the first time, her family wasn't
complaining about Annie being sticky.

In fact, they all seemed to enjoy being STUCK.